Grandaddy and Janetta

Grandaddy and Janetta

by Helen V. Griffith

pictures by James Stevenson

Greenwillow Books NEW YORK

Watercolor paints and a black pen were used
for the full-color art.
The text type is Perpetua.
Printed in Hong Kong by South China Printing Company (1988) Ltd.
First Edition   1 2 3 4 5 6 7 8 9 10

Library of Congress Cataloging-in-Publication Data

Griffith, Helen V.
     Grandaddy and Janetta / by Helen V. Griffith;
pictures by James Stevenson.
          p.   cm.
     Summary: Janetta enjoys her visit to her grandfather,
including such highlights as listening to the night
insects make music and admiring his cat's
new kittens.
     ISBN 0-688-11226-9 (trade). ISBN 0-688-11227-7 (lib.)
     [1. Grandfathers—Fiction.]
I. Stevenson, James, (date) ill.
II. Title.   PZ7.G8823Gp   1993
[E]—dc20   91-47707   CIP   AC

For Susan the Inspirer

CHAPTER ONE

Momma put Janetta on the train in Baltimore.

"Be sure you mind your grandaddy," she called after her.

But Janetta was too excited to listen. She found her seat and grinned out the window at Momma. They waved until the train started. Then they blew kisses until they couldn't see each other anymore. Janetta leaned back against her seat and watched Baltimore rush past the window.

The conductor came for her ticket. "So you're going all the way to Georgia," he said.

"I'm going to visit my grandaddy," said Janetta.

The conductor smiled down at her. "Well, your grandaddy's got a treat coming," he said. He took her ticket and put her bag on the overhead rack.

At first it was fun to sit watching buildings and highways and rivers flash by. Then Janetta started to feel an empty feeling inside herself. She opened the snack bag Momma had given her and ate half a jelly sandwich and three cookies. After that she felt full and empty at the same time. She began to wonder what Momma was doing. I bet she misses me, Janetta thought. She felt so sorry for Momma that tears came to her eyes and ran right down her face.

The conductor saw the tears. "Are you sick, little girl?" he asked.

"No," Janetta said. "I'm thinking how lonely my momma is."

"Where's your momma?" the conductor asked.

"She's home," Janetta said, "and she's never been away from me before."

"I don't think your momma's lonely," the conductor said. "She's too busy thinking about what a good time you and your grandaddy are going to have together."

Janetta's lip quivered. "It's been a whole year since I saw my grandaddy," she said. "I don't even remember what he looks like."

"A year's no time," the conductor said. "Once when I was a boy I didn't see my grandaddy for five years. But when I finally saw him, I knew him right away."

Janetta sniffed. "Right away?" she asked.

"Even though he had gone bald in the meantime," said the conductor.

"Grandaddy's bald already," Janetta said.

"Then you've got nothing to worry about," said the conductor.

"But maybe he's grown a beard," Janetta said.

The conductor laughed. "You'll know him," he said. "But even if you didn't, he would know you."

"I'm a lot bigger than I was last year," said Janetta, "and my hair is longer."

"In the five years that I didn't see my grandaddy," the conductor said, "I grew ten inches and gained twenty pounds and grew my hair down to my shoulders. But my grandaddy knew me."

"He did?" Janetta asked.

"He sure did," the conductor said. "He walked right up to me and looked me in the eye and said, 'You need a haircut.' And I looked right back and said, 'Well, you don't.'"

He and Janetta both laughed, and Janetta noticed that the empty feeling had gone away. A sleepy feeling had taken its place.

"Pleasant dreams," the conductor said. "We'll be in Georgia before you know it."

CHAPTER TWO

When they got to Georgia, Janetta grabbed her bag and hopped off the train, and there was Grandaddy. Janetta knew him right away.

"Grandaddy," she said, "you don't have a beard."

Grandaddy felt his chin. "Don't recall I ever did," he said.

"I was afraid you would have a beard, and I wouldn't recognize you," Janetta told him.

"That's funny," Grandaddy said. "I worried about the same thing. I thought to myself, if that child has grown a beard, how will I ever know her? I'll have to walk up to every bearded child that gets off the train and say, 'Are you Janetta?' until I find the right one."

"Grandaddy!" Janetta laughed. "Children don't have beards."

Grandaddy shook his head. "All that worrying for nothing," he said. He took Janetta's bag, and they walked alongside the tracks until they came to Grandaddy's place.

Janetta looked around carefully to make sure nothing had changed. The house was still old and small, and the yard was still mostly bare red dirt. The broken-down shed was still there, and so was the mule. It came running across the yard, heading straight for Janetta.

Janetta wasn't scared at all, even when the mule pushed against her with its big soft nose.

"Hello, Star," said Janetta.

"He remembers that you named him," Grandaddy said. "He's proud of that name."

Some chickens were pecking in the dirt.

"Grandaddy," Janetta asked, "are they the same chickens as last year?"

"Well, the eggs taste the same," said Grandaddy.

Then Janetta noticed that something was missing. "Where's the cat?" she asked.

"Around here someplace," said Grandaddy.

Janetta called, "Here, kitty, kitty." She waited for the cat to come running, but it didn't.

"Do you think the cat has forgotten me?" she asked.

"Nothing here has forgotten you," said Grandaddy.

Janetta was glad of that. But where is the cat? she wondered to herself.

CHAPTER THREE

It was raining. Janetta sat at the table by the window and watched puddles form in the bare red dirt. The mule looked out of the shed door, shook its head, and went back inside. The chickens perched on the porch rail with their feathers fluffed out and their eyes half shut. There was no sign of the cat.

Grandaddy put an old checkerboard and checkers on the table. "This was your momma's," he said.

Janetta hadn't played checkers in a long while but she remembered how, so they started to play.

After a while, Grandaddy said, "It was raining like this the day the mule and I planned our trip."

Janetta looked up. "What trip?" she asked.

"The mule got it into its head that it wanted to see the whole United States of America," Grandaddy said.

"How could you tell it wanted that?" Janetta asked.

"Me and that mule are close," said Grandaddy. "So I took a map out to the shed and we looked it over, and the next day off we went."

"Walking?" Janetta asked.

"Well, the mule walked and I rode," said Grandaddy. "We left at sunup and we got home just at dark."

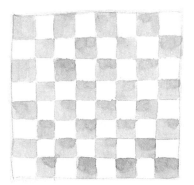

"The same day?" Janetta asked.

"The mule is fast," Grandaddy explained, "and not much interested in sightseeing."

"Grandaddy," Janetta said, "you can't see the whole United States in one day."

"We did, though," Grandaddy said proudly. "All forty-eight of them."

"Grandaddy," Janetta said, "there are fifty states."

Grandaddy opened his eyes wide. "You don't say so!" he said.

"I learned it in school," said Janetta.

"Well, don't tell the mule," Grandaddy said. "It thinks it saw them all."

Janetta and Grandaddy went back to their game.

After a while Janetta said, "Grandaddy, if you and the mule ever go to visit the states you missed, I want to come along."

"Wouldn't go without you," said Grandaddy. "And neither would the mule."

CHAPTER FOUR

At night Grandaddy and Janetta sat out on the steps and watched the day finish up. As the sky darkened and the stars appeared, the air became full of sound. There were clicks and rattles and clacks and sweet high trills.

"What a racket," Janetta said.

"That's music," said Grandaddy. "Listen."

Janetta listened. She heard *treep, treep.*

"Cricket," said Grandaddy.

Janetta heard *bre-e-e-e.*

"Tree frog," said Grandaddy.

Janetta heard *katydid, katydid.*

"Katydid saying its name," said Grandaddy.

"Katydid looks just like a flying leaf."

"I'd like to see that," Janetta said.

Grandaddy and Janetta sat and listened to the music.

After a while Grandaddy said, "It's my turn now." He pulled his mouth organ out of his pocket and blew into it, sliding it back and forth across his lips.

The sounds around them stopped.

"They're listening," Grandaddy said. He began to play an old-time song. "You can sing it if you know the words," he said to Janetta.

"Do the insects sing along?" Janetta asked.

"They dance," said Grandaddy. "They're down there now, dancing in the grass."

Grandaddy went back to playing his mouth organ.

Janetta looked down into a little patch of grass.

She couldn't see any insects dancing or any tree frogs, either.

Suddenly a green leaf flew up and landed on the step.

"Katydid," said Grandaddy, between notes.

The katydid flew off the step and vanished in the dark.

"Katydid invites you to dance," said Grandaddy.

Janetta was glad for the invitation, because the music did make her feel like dancing. "But I don't want to step on your friends," she said.

"You won't," said Grandaddy. "They're quick."

So Janetta jumped down to the ground and began dancing to the mouth organ music. She hopped and wiggled and spun around until she was out of breath. Then she sat back down on the step beside Grandaddy. "I didn't know I was such a good dancer," she said.

"You're better than the bugs," said Grandaddy. He shook his mouth organ and put it back in his pocket.

"Thank you, Grandaddy," said Janetta. "You are, too."

CHAPTER FIVE

In the morning Janetta went out to visit the mule before breakfast.

The mule was back in a corner, staring at something in the hay. Janetta went over and looked. There was the cat—and not just the cat.

Janetta ran out of the shed and into the house. "Grandaddy!" she shouted. "The cat has had kittens."

Grandaddy nodded. "They do that," he said.

"I thought it was a boy," said Janetta.

"Used to think that myself," said Grandaddy. "But the cat knew better."

Janetta ran back out to the shed. She and the mule examined the kittens. Janetta held each kitten up, and the mule snuffled it with its nose. One of the kittens had a little white star-shaped mark on its forehead.

"Look, Star," Janetta said to the mule. "This kitten takes after you."

The mule gave it another snuffle.

Janetta put the kitten back with its mother. Then she ran to the house and sat down to breakfast with Grandaddy.

"Grandaddy," she said, "there's a kitten out there with a star on its head, and it's the mule's favorite."

"How can you tell that?" Grandaddy asked.

"It got the most snuffles," Janetta said.

"A sure sign," said Grandaddy.

Janetta sat stirring her oatmeal. "Grandaddy," she said, "what are you going to do with the kittens?"

"Haven't thought," said Grandaddy.

Janetta stirred her oatmeal round and round in the bowl. "Grandaddy," she said, "what if somebody came here and said, 'I'm looking for kittens, and I hear you have some'?"

"I'd say, 'Help yourself,'" said Grandaddy.

"Oh," said Janetta.

"Yep," Grandaddy said. "I'd say, 'Help yourself, but you can't have the one with the star on its head, because that's my mule's favorite.'"

Janetta laughed and started in on her oatmeal. "Guess what, Grandaddy," she said. "The mule's favorite kitten is my favorite, too."

CHAPTER SIX

Grandaddy and Janetta were sitting on the steps, shelling peas. The mule was standing in the shade, switching flies off its back with its tail. Every now and then Janetta threw it a podful of peas. The chickens were pecking around in the dirt. Every now and then Janetta threw them some peas, too.

The cat led her kittens out of the shed and into the yard. The kittens got busy pouncing on insects and stalking the chickens and batting the peapods.

"Grandaddy," Janetta said, "I've been thinking about a name for my favorite kitten."

"What's it to be?" asked Grandaddy.

"Well, I'd like to call it Star," Janetta said.

"Good idea," said Grandaddy.

"But that's the mule's name, too," Janetta said. "We might get them mixed up."

Grandaddy thought about it. "It could happen," he said. "I might set out milk for Star, and it would be the mule and he'd put his big foot right in the bowl. Or I'd hitch up Star to the plow, and it would be the kitten and plowing with a kitten is slow work." Grandaddy shook his head. "No, you'd better not name it Star," he said.

"But what else can you call a kitten with a star on its head?" Janetta asked.

"It's a problem, all right," said Grandaddy.

The two of them shelled peas and thought.

"Only one thing to do," Grandaddy said finally. "Get rid of the kitten."

Janetta stopped shelling peas. "Grandaddy!" she said.

"Well, we can't have two Stars around here," said Grandaddy, "and I need the mule."

"But, Grandaddy," Janetta said, "the kitten is so little."

Grandaddy kept shelling peas.

"And it's shy," Janetta said.

Grandaddy kept on shelling peas.

"And it's used to us," Janetta said.

Grandaddy stopped shelling peas and looked at Janetta. "Think it could get used to Baltimore?" he asked.

Janetta stared at Grandaddy. Then she jumped to her feet, scattering peapods everywhere and sending the kittens running for their mother. "I know it could, Grandaddy," she said.

"That's that, then," said Grandaddy, and he went back to shelling peas.

Janetta was so happy that she threw a big handful of peas to the mule. Then she threw peas to the chickens. She threw some peas to the kittens, too.

"Did I mention these peas were for dinner?" Grandaddy asked.

Janetta giggled and sat back down beside him.

"That's a good idea, Grandaddy," she said, "for me to take the kitten home."

"It came to me just like that," said Grandaddy.

"Now I'll have a Star, and you'll have a Star," Janetta said.

"Sure enough," said Grandaddy.

"And Momma will have the kitten for company while I'm away," Janetta said, "so I can come to see you twice as often."

"Now that," said Grandaddy, "is the best idea yet." He dropped the last of the peas into the pot and threw the pods out for the chickens to fight over.

Then Grandaddy and Janetta went inside to cook what was left of the peas for dinner.